FLAMBOYAN

Story by **Arnold Adoff**   Pictures by **Karen Barbour**

Harcourt Brace Jovanovich, Publishers

San Diego   New York   London

Text copyright © 1988 by Arnold Adoff

Illustrations copyright © 1988 by Karen Barbour

Requests for permission to make copies of any
part of the work should be mailed to:
Permissions, Harcourt Brace Jovanovich, Publishers,
Orlando, Florida 32887.

Library of Congress Cataloging-in-Publication Data

Adoff, Arnold.

Flamboyan/by Arnold Adoff; pictures by Karen Barbour.—1st ed.

p. cm.

Summary: One sunny afternoon while everyone is resting, Flamboyan, a young girl named after the tree
whose red blossoms are the same color as her hair, dreamily flies over her Caribbean island home.

ISBN 0-15-228404-4

[1. Flight—Fiction. 2. Caribbean area—Fiction.] I. Barbour, Karen, ill. II. Title.

PZ7.A2616F1   1988

[E]—dc19   87-35909

Printed in the United States of America   First edition   A B C D E

The illustrations in this book were done in Winsor & Newton watercolors and gouache on
140-lb. Arches cold-press paper.
The text type was set in ITC Benguiat Book by Central Graphics, San Diego, California.
Color separations were made by Heinz Weber, Inc., Los Angeles, California.
Printed by Holyoke Lithograph, Springfield, Massachusetts
Bound by Horowitz/Rae Book Manufacturers, Inc., Fairfield, New Jersey
Production supervision by Warren Wallerstein and Ginger Boyer
Designed by Nancy J. Ponichtera

**For the girls and boys of the
island of Culebra, Puerto Rico**

—A. A.

For Susan and Steve

—K. B.

One sunshine morning, in the month of July,
on a small green island in the blue Caribbean sea,
a baby girl is born.

The baby has a beautiful brown face.   Her hair 🍂 is the color
of the flame red blossoms 🍂 on the Flamboyan tree, 🍂 so bright and red
they catch the sunlight, 🍂 and seem to burn 🍂 outside the window of her room.
    The baby has soft skin, 🍂 the color of the bark 🍂 of the tree.   Her legs and arms
are as strong and round 🍂 as the branches of that Flamboyan tree.

Her mother and father name her Flamboyan, 🍃 because of her flame red hair,
and because the girl Flamboyan will always see that tree 🍃 through her window,
through sunshine mornings 🍃 or raining afternoons, 🍃 as she grows through the seasons
of her early years, 🍃 through the seasons of the years 🍃 of the Flamboyan tree;
until she is a tall and strong young girl, 🍃 and the tree is a tall and strong young tree.

Soon Flamboyan is a growing girl, ✐ brown as tree bark, ✐ eyes as big
as two round stones ✐ staring up from the bottom ✐ of her shallow wading place.
    Each morning, ✐ the rooster wakes her before six, ✐ and she is out of bed
and out of the house ✐ in three fast steps, ✐ as the rooster crows his noisy invitation
to the rising morning sun, ✐ and the sparkling water of the shallow wading place.

Her legs shine, 🍃 wet with sparkling water.   She washes 🍃 and runs 🍃 and plays
with schools of shining silver fish.
    Each morning, 🍃 in the early sun, 🍃 she raises her arms over her head
and looks up 🍃 into the open sky.   Two pelicans fly over her head, 🍃 following the silver fish
out to the open sea, 🍃 for their shining 🍃 breakfast 🍃 invitation.

The trees grow their branches 🍃 up to the open sky, 🍃 and Flamboyan can reach her own arms up to that sky 🍃 and watch the pelicans fly, 🍃 and follow the silver fish.

Standing on the green grass ground 🍃 or in the shallow wading place,
she feels rooted, 🍃 like the trees.   But Flamboyan knows she is free
as birds in the open sky.

With 🍃 open 🍃 eyes 🍃 🍃 she dreams 🍃 to 🍃 fly.

Each day, 🍂 under the cool umbrella of Flamboyan branches and leaves and flowers, the young girl 🍂 braids her long red hair.   The breeze brings the sound of a skillet clanking the top of the kitchen stove.

It is an early morning song: 🍂 her own breakfast invitation.

Flamboyan turns to home.   She begins the day.

Out in her yard, ✍ Flamboyan fills the pans with water, ✍ then scatters chicken feed
around the chicken house.   Roosters and hens and baby chicks follow along
in the early morning ✍ girl-and-chicken dance.
      She searches the nests ✍ and brings her basket, ✍ full of fresh eggs, ✍ into the house.

Her mother is in the kitchen, 🍂 and there are thick slices of toasted bread with butter and honey, 🍂 for breakfast; 🍂 and a cup of warm milk, 🍂 flavored with a little coffee 🍂 from the bubbling pot.

Her father is up before first light, ✎ before the rooster and Flamboyan.

He leaves on his bicycle ✎ in the last of the dark ✎ to ride into the town, to his job with the electric company.   Her father is the electric expert.   He brings power to the people.   When there is trouble with any electric lines, ✎ he can climb high poles ✎ to make the system work.

Early each morning, ✎ Flamboyan and her mother travel the busy beach road, selling oranges ✎ that grow on their yard trees, ✎ and coconut candies they make each evening before bed.

When the sun is high, 🍂 almost to noon, 🍂 Flamboyan and her mother begin to walk the beach road back home.   Even though the sun is very strong, 🍂 Flamboyan looks up to the sky 🍂 at birds and clouds, 🍂 and the tops of trees.

Sometimes she finds papaya or mangoes 🍂 on trees that grow along their way.

Sometimes there are longhorned cows 🍂 blocking the road, 🍂 chewing the mesquite that grows everywhere.

They see friends, 🍂 some neighbors, 🍂 along the way.   As they walk, 🍂 her mother and her friends pass the island news of the day 🍂 back and forth.

But Flamboyan is listening to the sounds 🍂 of the sea gulls flying over her head.

The tree grows its branches 🍃 up to the open sky,
and Flamboyan sits rooted to the ground, like her tree.
But she feels free 🍃 as any bird 🍃 in the open sky.
With 🍃 open 🍃 eyes 🍃 🍃 she 🍃 dreams 🍃 to 🍃 fly.

Flamboyan looks up 🍃 into the center of a bright red bloom.

Now Flamboyan is not rooted.   She begins to move.   She is moving
on the warm whisper breeze.   First her long red hair stirs.   Then her face
lifts to the center of the flower.   She smells its sweetness, 🍃 and the salt sea smell
above the tree.   Her arms lift 🍃 into the warm breeze.   She stretches strong arms

and shoulders upward, and then she is standing.   Flamboyan is rising 🍃 above
the green grass ground.   She is rising into the umbrella of brilliant flowers
above the rooted tree.   Flamboyan is rising into the salt sea smell 🍃 above
her Flamboyan tree.

   She is rising above the warm whisper breeze, 🍃 into clouds, 🍃 and high blue skies.

   She 🍃 🍃 moves 🍃 🍃 rises 🍃 🍃 flies.

Flamboyan flies.

    She flies over her house ✎ and says ✎ "sleep tight"
to her mother ✎ napping in the bedroom.

    She flies over her street ✎ and says ✎ "be well" ✎ to the friends ✎ and neighbors
in their houses down below.

    She flies out beyond her street, ✎ past the town ✎ to the beach road,
and looks down ✎ on the longhorned cows of William Martinez.

She flies over his favorite horse, ✐ tied to a mesquite tree ✐ at the side of the road,
and over William, ✐ reading in tree shade.

Flamboyan flies over the fresh water lagoon, ✐ home to land birds ✐ like sparrows,
and pigeons, ✐ and doves; ✐ and home to sea birds ✐ like gulls, ✐ and terns, ✐ and pelicans;
all drinking and splashing ✐ in the cool sweet water.

She flies over her favorite mangrove shore, 🍂 and over the baby birds
splashing in the tall red mangrove roots 🍂 at the edge of the water.
   There is a sudden rush of wings, 🍂 and all the birds rise up 🍂 in a great cloud
of noise and wind and feathers, 🍂 to surround Flamboyan in the air.

The birds circle and fly and dive, 🌿 then glide back down 🌿 to the fresh water lagoon.
Some come to rest 🌿 on tops of coconut palm trees.   Some splash back into the water.
Baby birds squawk hungry in the mangrove roots.

Flamboyan is feeding with the sugar birds, 🖋 those gold and yellow honeysuckers.
She is darting down with the flycatchers.   She is racing the frigate birds
just above the sandy shore.   She hops along the beach with the sooty tern.
    She calls with the mangrove cuckoos.   She coos with Paloma Turka, 🖋 the doves
that circle the hillside trees.   She soars and glides the air currents with giant kingfisher,
until she is higher than warm whisper breezes and salt sea smells.
    Flamboyan flies and dives into Dakity Bay.   She flies 🖋 and dives 🖋 and flies 🖋 with the pelicans
following 🖋 🖋 the 🖋 🖋 silver 🖋 🖋 fish.

Flamboyan is flying above the white cap waves.   She blows with the warm breezes
and salt sea smells, 🍃 back along the beach road, 🍃 to her town.

She whispers past cool shaded porches, 🍃 and over yards of periwinkle
and bird of paradise flowers, 🍃 and along bougainvillea vines growing on stone walls.

Flamboyan glides on a whisper of sweet scents 🍃 from wild orchids
and flowering lemon trees, 🍃 through this summer afternoon.

Now she rides on a gray cloud, 🍃 in a sudden rain shower, 🍃 down to the roofs
of friends and neighbors.

Flamboyan falls gently onto her own roof.

She feels as small as a single drop of water, 🍃 falling into 🍃 the very center
of a brilliant red flower, 🍃 blooming in the umbrella of her own Flamboyan tree.

It is the end of the afternoon.   It is the end of the day.

Flamboyan sits on the green grass ground ⚡ under her favorite tree, ⚡ at the side of her house, ⚡ in her yard.   The thick trunk fits right into the shape of her back.

The brilliant red and orange flame flowers ⚡ move in the warm whisper breezes of this late afternoon time.   The last rays of late sun ⚡ warm her cheeks and ears.

The sun continues to slowly set.   It touches the top trees ⚡ on the top ridge of the hills, ⚡ above her street and her town.

The sun slides down the trees, ♪ little by little, ♪ then slides into the trees, and finally slides under the trees, ♪ until the sun is behind these trees, behind the ridge, ♪ behind the hills.   Now ♪ ♪ it ♪ is ♪ ♪ twilight.

It is almost dark.   The cool evening breeze ♪ brings the sound of a dinner pot clanking the top of the kitchen stove.   Flamboyan can hear her father and mother sharing their stories ♪ of the day.

It is time for dinner, ♪ time for food and talk.

Flamboyan pulls a bright red flame flower 🍃 from the umbrella of blooms above her head.
She pushes its curving stem 🍃 behind her ear 🍃 and smiles up into the evening sky.
    She will always see that tree 🍃 through sunshine mornings 🍃 or raining
afternoons 🍃 as she grows 🍃 and as she flies through the seasons of Flamboyan.

    Now 🍃 she 🍃 gets 🍃 up 🍃 🍃 and 🍃 walks 🍃 🍃 into 🍃 her 🍃 house.